And Then It Happened
..3..

AND THEN IT HAPPENED

3

M & L Wade

Books for Boys

ISBN 0-9731178-2-6

Printed in Canada

Books for Boys
P.O. Box 87
Strathroy ON N7G 3J1

Ha! Ha!
You've been officially pranked
by Gordon!

Contents

Chapter 1

Attack of the Scarecrow

Halloween was just three days away, and this year, Gordon, Paulo and I were especially eager. After having spent last Halloween lost in a cornfield and coming home completely candy-less, we were more determined than ever to go trick-or-treating. This year, we would be trick-or-treating in my neighbourhood to make sure we couldn't possibly get lost.

The entire town was decorated with pumpkins, scarecrows and tombstones. Some new people had moved in down the street from my house a few months earlier, and while we had never seen the new people, they did have an amazing Halloween display on their front lawn - the scariest, meanest-looking life-size scarecrow I've ever seen. It seemed like everyone in town, kids and adults alike, were talking about this scary scarecrow. Everyone agreed it was the best Halloween decoration they'd ever seen. That's when Gordon and I got the idea that it might be fun to play a joke on the new people.

Right after supper that day, we met as planned in the shadows next door to the scarecrow. The new people's house was in complete darkness; it appeared as if no one were home. *Perfect*, I thought as we jumped the fence and stood looking up at the great scarecrow. Up close it appeared even scarier. Gordon and I set to work.

*　　　*　　　*

The next morning as Gordon and I walked to school, we noticed all the kids pointing to the scarecrow and laughing. Cars were slowing down to get a better look, and some even stopped in the middle of the road. Gordon and I joined in the laughter. It seemed as though our little joke was a hit. The scarecrow was turned around with his back to the street. His pants were down around his ankles, and he was "mooning" the entire neighbourhood.

On our way home from school later that day, we saw that the scarecrow had been put back to rights and was staring out menacingly at the street once again. *Someone must be home after all*, I thought.

Once again after dinner, Gordon and I met outside after dusk. This time I carefully watched the house to see if anyone was inside. All was dark and quiet. We hopped the fence and went to work. Just as we were finishing the job, I looked over my shoulder in time to see a curtain moving inside the house.

"Gordon!" I whispered. "I think somebody's home. Let's get outta here!"

We gathered up our empty bags and took off into the darkness.

The next morning there were even more cars and people laughing at our creation. Gone were the scarecrow's own clothes, and there he stood, in one of Gordon's mother's old dresses and a blond wig. In his hands was a sign that said "Kisses - 25¢ each".

On the walk home from school that day, we were not too surprised to see that the dress and wig had been removed, and the scarecrow was dressed in his own clothes again.

That night, I showed up before Gordon arrived to get a good look at the house. Someone *had* to be in there, and that someone must be watching us. Then I heard Gordon coming down the street carrying a bag in each hand that clanked loudly with every step he took.

"Shhhh," I warned. "Someone may be home."

"Nah," said Gordon. "The house is totally dark. Don't worry so much."

We set to work. Gordon had raided all the recycling boxes on his street that morning, and he brought with him twenty-four empty beer bottles and several wine and whiskey bottles. We spread the bottles around the feet of the scarecrow, tilted his hat at a funny angle, and taped an empty beer bottle in his hand. We stood back to admire our work, and then I saw it. A shadow crossed in front of one of the windows inside the dark house, and the curtain definitely moved. Gordon saw it, too.

"Let's get out of here before we get caught," he said, and we scrambled back over the fence.

When I awoke the next morning, I could hardly contain my excitement. It was Halloween. This year, there was going to be a costume contest at school, so we were supposed to wear our costumes. I quickly pulled on my Leafs jersey and jeans, and ran downstairs. As I was eating breakfast, there was a knock at the door. I opened it and froze. There stood my teacher, Mrs. Hoagsbrith!

"Hi," I said weakly. "What are you doing here?" *Boy, I must really be in trouble if the teacher is making house-calls*, I thought.

Mrs. Hoagsbrith burst out laughing and said, "Ha! Fooled you, didn't I? It's me, Gordon!"

I opened my eyes wide to get a better look. I couldn't believe it. Gordon had come up with some great costumes in the past, but this was his best yet. He was dressed in a red and white polka-dot dress, identical to the one the real Mrs. Hoagsbrith wore every Friday. He had on a grey wig, high-heeled shoes, pantyhose, and around his neck hung a pair of black glasses on a silver chain. He had tied a pillow to his rear-end and held it in place with a wide belt, and he had stuffed two entire boxes of tissues into one of his mother's bras. Except for being a little bit shorter, Gordon was a dead-ringer for our teacher. He even carried a purse and wore make-up.

"Wow!" was all I could think to say.

On the way to school, kids kept stopping and looking at us. They, too, were fooled by Gordon's costume and wondered why I was walking to school with Mrs. Hoagsbrith. They whispered and pointed until we got to the new people's house, and then they forgot about me and the teacher and laughed out loud at the "drunk" scarecrow.

We met Paulo at school. Paulo always had great costumes. Both of his parents helped him to make whatever he wanted to be. This year, he was dressed as an astronaut, complete with a round glass helmet (an old fish bowl) and an oxygen tank on his back. All attention, however, was on Gordon. Kids gathered around him admiring his costume and laughing as Gordon did his best imitation of our teacher.

When the bell rang, Gordon stood at the front of the line, impersonating Mrs. Hoagsbrith.

"I am your teacher, *Mrs. Hog's breath*," he squeaked in a high voice. Suddenly, he felt a tap on his shoulder and turned to face the real teacher, looking tired and worn-out already, and it was only nine o'clock.

The day seemed to drag on. We watched Halloween videos, carved pumpkins, and paraded around the gym in our costumes. Gordon won the prize for the most imaginative costume. Paulo won for the best home-made costume. I, as usual, won nothing, but it didn't matter, because tonight I was going to go trick-or-treating and get more candy than ever before!

Paulo walked home from school with Gordon and me to my house. When we got to the new people's house, we were surprised to see that the scarecrow was no longer in the front yard. It was gone.

"Gee," I said. "I hope the new people aren't too mad at us. After all, we were just having a little fun." As we turned to go, a shiver ran down my spine, and I had the awful feeling that someone was watching us.

7

We hurried through dinner and waited for it to get dark so we could begin trick-or-treating.

"Be careful," my mom said. "Don't eat anything until we can check it, and be home by 8:30. Not a minute later."

Finally, it was dark enough, and we headed off.

"Let's check out the new people's place," said Gordon. "I wonder if the scarecrow is back, or if anyone is home handing out candy."

"I don't know," I said, a little worried.

"Aw, come on," said Paulo, leading the way up the sidewalk. A moment later, we stood in front of the house, which was dark except for a tiny pumpkin which glowed on the front porch.

"See," said Gordon. "Someone's home."

"Yeah, but the scarecrow's gone. The new people could be really mad at us," I said.

"Only one way to find out!" said Gordon, and he bravely marched up the front steps and rang the doorbell, with Paulo and me behind him.

We waited for a full minute, and Gordon rang the bell

again. No one answered. We turned around to leave, and Paulo gasped,

"Look, guys! The scarecrow's back! It wasn't there a minute ago!"

Sure enough, the big scarecrow was back on its perch.

"Let's cut through the bushes," I said nervously.

"Chicken!" shouted Gordon, jumping off the porch and running over to the scarecrow to investigate.

And then it happened. The scarecrow jumped off the haystack it had been standing on, let out a piercing scream, and lunged toward Gordon! Gordon leapt out of the way and began running, with Paulo and me right behind him. Gordon stumbled along in his high heels and Paulo and I quickly overtook him. In an instant, the scarecrow caught up to him, grabbing wildly at his dress.

"LET ME GO!" screamed Gordon, struggling to get away. He twisted and pulled, and then we heard the sound of popping buttons and tearing fabric, and Gordon came racing toward us wearing nothing but his mother's bra and pantyhose. Kicking off his high-heels, he quickly caught up to Paulo and me.

We raced past my house, where my mother was handing out candy to a group of little kids.

"Mom!" I yelled. "Call the police!"

Mom waved and said, "Slow down, boys. You have plenty of time to get lots of candy."

On we raced. We saw my neighbour, Mr. Butterworth, handing out candy on his front porch.

"Mr. Butterworth! HELP!!" I hollered.

"Oh, you kids! Up to more pranks again? Who's your big friend?"

I looked over my shoulder to see the scarecrow right behind us.

"We have to hide," I panted.

"Run to the schoolyard!" hissed Paulo.

We dashed down the street and into the dark schoolyard. We hid in the shadows among the playground equipment, and it looked as though we had lost the scarecrow. He hadn't followed us into the schoolyard.

"Where is he?" panted Gordon.

"I d-don't know," I nervously replied.

We waited for what seemed like hours in the dark schoolyard.

"We have to make a run for your place," said Paulo.

"He could still be lurking out there somewhere," argued Gordon. "And I don't want to die in a bra and pantyhose!"

"Well, we can't stay here all night," I said. "Come on."

With pounding hearts, we crept to the bushes at the edge of the schoolyard. I nervously peered around them. The coast was clear.

"Come on!" I whispered.

Ducking in the shadows, we hurried along the edge of the schoolyard until we came to the sidewalk. There were still a few trick-or-treaters far down at the other end of the street.

"Run!" I shouted.

We raced to my house, up the driveway, and threw open the front door. We stumbled into the house, hearts pounding and breathing hard. Gordon slammed the door behind us.

"That was close!" he panted.

"Who *was* that? Some maniac on the loose? We gotta call the police!" said Paulo.

Just then, the front door was thrown open, and the giant scarecrow flew into the house, laughing like a madman. He grabbed Gordon and Paulo. I screamed and ran down the hall, where I collided with my parents coming out of the kitchen.

"Oh, sweetie, you're home!" my mother said. "And I see you boys have met our new neighbour - the Chief of Police!!"

My parents and the new neighbour, dressed up like a scarecrow, laughed out loud as Gordon, Paulo and I stood there, our mouths open in shock.

"You mean you were in on it?" I stammered. "You knew this guy was gonna chase us and *you let him?*"

"Well, it seemed only fair," said my father. "After what you and Gordon did to his scarecrow!"

I couldn't believe it. My parents had beaten us at our own game. I vowed right then and there never to pull another prank again as long as I lived!

Chapter 2

Gordon's Invention

We were sitting in our clubhouse in my backyard one day when Gordon suddenly exclaimed,

"I've got a great idea, and it's going to make us rich!"

"What is it?" demanded Paulo.

"Recycled Kleenex!" cried Gordon.

"Nobody would buy that!" shouted Paulo.

"Gross!" I added. "Gees, where do you get these ideas from anyway?"

Gordon had always been a little strange. One day in

13

Kindergarten, he drank different colours of paint. When the teacher caught him and asked why he did it, he told her he wanted to pee different colours.

"Just kidding about the Kleenex, guys. But listen to this. This invention will make us so much money, we'll be able to hire the teacher to do our homework. In fact, we'll be so rich, we can hire her to clean our rooms, too!" Gordon took a deep breath and paused for dramatic effect. "What we're going to invent is *The Super Slider Snow Suit!*"

"The *what*?" I asked, puzzled.

"The Super Slider Snow Suit!" he repeated. "We'll get all of our old crazy carpets and cut them up and staple them to make a complete suit. Instead of just *sitting* on a crazy carpet to go tobogganing, our *bodies* will be toboggans! Every kid will want one!"

It was an excellent idea. We spent the next couple of hours cutting, gluing and stapling until we had made three Super Slider Suits. We tried them on and modelled them for each other. They fit perfectly.

"Let's go try 'em out!" shouted Gordon.

Our town has a huge hill in the park where all the kids go tobogganing. At the foot of the hill there is a big skating rink which is always crowded with hockey players on Saturdays. When we got there, it seemed as though half the kids in town were there enjoying the perfect tobogganing conditions. People whizzed down the hill and then lugged their sleds, flying saucers and magic carpets back up. Gordon, Paulo and I were the only kids not pulling something up the hill with us. We were *wearing* our toboggans!

When we got to the top, everyone crowded around us to admire our Super Slider Snow Suits. Like models, we posed for our fans. Then we were ready to try out our invention. We walked to the edge of the hill like astronauts getting ready to board the Space Shuttle. On the count of three, we ran the last few steps and launched our bodies over the side of the hill. Down the icy hill we flew on our stomachs.

Sometimes in life things don't turn out as you had planned. Then there are times when things go *better* than you had planned. This was one of those times! We streaked down the hill at the speed of light, completely out of control. Normally when you go tobogganing and things get out of hand, you can always roll off your sleigh and come to a messy stop in the snow. However, when you're *wearing* your toboggan, you *can't* roll off. You are at the mercy of the hill, and this hill had no mercy at all. We felt every bump, lump and stump as we sped down the hill. The cruel hill twisted and spun us around and aimed us directly toward the skating rink at the bottom! Like corks flying out of a champagne bottle, we shot onto the ice directly into the path of the hockey players, knocking them down like bowling pins. There was shouting and yelling and cursing as we slid from one end of the rink to the other, crash-landing into the hockey net at the opposite end, taking the goalie with us. When the stars disappeared and the bells in our ears stopped ringing, we slowly and painfully crawled out of the net and got to our feet, testing all of our joints and muscles to see if anything was broken. It was then that we noticed the crowd of angry hockey players that surrounded us, blocking our exit. The words "Sorry" and "It was an accident!" poured from our mouths until the ferocious mob finally let us go.

Back at the clubhouse, we decided that Super Slider Snow Suits were too dangerous to sell and we'd have to think of another way to get rich. I guess we would just have to do our own homework and clean our own rooms in the meantime.

Chapter 3

Santa Claws

My best Christmas memory happened several years ago when Gordon, Paulo and I were still very young. Gordon's dad had taken the three of us to the mall to visit the jolly old elf. Anxiously, we stood in line with dozens of other toy-hungry kids waiting to tell Santa what we hoped to find under our trees this year. Gordon's father left us waiting in the long line while he did some last-minute shopping in the store across from Santa's castle.

The line slowly made its way forward until we were at

the front and could finally take our turns sitting on Santa's lap. We were all a little bit nervous - after all, this was Santa Claus, the man we waited for all year, the man we wrote letters to, the man we watched on TV.

One of Santa's helpers came forward, took Gordon by the hand and led him toward the Big Guy. She picked Gordon up and placed him gently on Santa's lap. And then it happened. Gordon accidentally (and very loudly) farted! Parents standing in line with their kids heard it and chuckled behind their hands. Santa's helpers heard it, too, and they quickly moved away from Santa and Gordon. Paulo and I heard it and were mortified! This was Santa Claus, the man you asked for toys, and Gordon had cut the cheese while sitting on his lap! I waited for Santa to give one of his famous HO! HO! HO!'s and just laugh it off, but Santa surprised everyone by roaring to life, jumping off his throne, cursing and flinging poor Gordon off his lap as if he were a rag doll! Gordon sailed through the air and crash-landed in a heap on the other side of the castle. Santa didn't stop there, either.

"I'VE HAD IT WITH BRATS LIKE YOU!" he

shouted, striding towards Gordon, who dodged for his life among the decorations and artificial Christmas trees.

At that moment, Gordon's dad stepped out of the store across the mall and glanced toward Santa's castle. No doubt he expected to see his son sitting calmly on Santa's lap reciting a long list of Christmas wishes and sharing a tender moment with the jolly old man. What he saw instead was a furious, raging man in a red suit chasing after his son, ready to beat him to a pulp! Dropping his parcels, Mr. Smith raced across the mall, climbed up the castle steps and began slugging it out with Santa Claus! Like two WWE fighters, the men kicked, punched and clawed at each other while horrified shoppers watched the scene, their mouths open and eyes popping. Santa grabbed Mr. Smith and pushed him into a large Christmas tree, knocking it over and smashing all the ornaments. Gordon's dad jumped up and grabbed a plastic life-size reindeer from the display. He threw it with all his might at Santa, knocking him head over heels into the big sleigh. Santa jumped up and charged at Mr. Smith, but Gordon's dad was quicker. Grabbing Santa's beard, he landed a hard punch squarely on Santa's face, knocking the man out cold.

Mothers clutched their children and hurried them out of the line-up. Several little kids started to cry.

Mall security had to be summoned, and for a moment they just stood there, staring at the scene dumbfounded. Then they sprang into action, grabbing Mr. Smith and dragging him, still kicking and cursing, toward the mall doors with Gordon, Paulo and me trailing behind them. Mr. Smith was flung into the parking lot and told that he was no longer welcome to shop in this mall, and that he ought to be ashamed of himself, beating up Santa Claus in front of all those innocent little children.

It was then that Gordon, Paulo and I learned the truth about Santa Claus. He wasn't just a jolly old elf who lived at the North Pole and brought presents to little kids. He didn't just slide down chimneys delivering gifts in the middle of the night. From that moment on, we knew the truth. Santa was a Sumo Wrestler.

Chapter 4

The Cursed Hat

It was early spring and the ice had just melted off of the lakes and rivers. Paulo's dad was taking the three of us up to his cabin by the lake for a weekend of fishing. Gordon and I shivered in the half-rain, half-snow at the end of my driveway as we waited for Mr. Lima and Paulo to pick us up. We were glad to finally see their van turn down my street and come to a stop in front of us. We threw our gear in and climbed in the back seat. I said hello to Paulo and his dad, and then I saw it. Mr. Lima was wearing his expensive, genuine beaver fur hat, his most prized possession. Gordon saw it, too, and he flashed me a nervous glance. Neither of us had seen the hat since the day we accidentally dropped it into the pig pen at the Lima farm and Gordon, Paulo and I had to jump into the stall to wrestle the hat away from the angry pig. When we finally recaptured it, we thought the hat had been ruined Fortunately for us, Mrs. Lima had come to our rescue and when she was finished cleaning the hat, it looked as good as new. To this day, she had kept our secret safe from Paulo's dad.

Mr. Lima greeted us cheerfully. "Good morning, boys. Ready to do some fishing? I hope you dressed warm. It'll be freezing cold by the lake. I've got this expensive, genuine beaver fur hat to keep me warm," he boasted proudly, pointing to the hat. "Bet you've never seen a hat like this before."

"No, never," lied Gordon. "It sure looks warm."

"And good looking," I added.

Mr. Lima beamed with pleasure. "It's too bad you

kids don't have an expensive, genuine beaver fur hat. But your wool toques will have to do, I guess."

Two hours later we arrived at the cabin. After dropping off our gear, we spent the rest of the afternoon on the lake. The fishing was great, but oh, so cold. I have to admit that Mr. Lima did look warm in his expensive, genuine beaver fur hat. Gordon, Paulo and I shivered as the wind blew through our thin toques while we trolled around the frigid lake. We were still shivering a few hours later when we returned with our fish to the cabin. Gordon, Paulo and I huddled around the wood stove, trying to warm up, as Mr. Lima, still wearing the beaver fur hat, cleaned the fish and made dinner. He wasn't cold in the least. We eventually warmed up, ate a wonderful fish dinner, and played card games 'till bedtime.

It was three o'clock in the morning when I woke up, warm and snug in my sleeping bag, with the uncomfortable knowledge that I had to use the bathroom - right away. The only problem was that there was no bathroom, only a cold outhouse fifty metres behind the cabin. Sighing, I slid out of my bunk so as not to wake

Gordon or Paulo, found my flashlight, and pulled on my pants and shirt. I tiptoed down the hall and past the room where Mr. Lima lay snoring loudly in his sleep. I took my coat off the hook by the back door and slid into my boots. As I reached for my toque, I saw it. There it was on a hook next to my thin wool toque - Mr. Lima's expensive, genuine beaver fur hat. I stared at it for a moment. The wind howled outside the cabin, and I knew how cold a trip to the outhouse could be. But, if I wore Mr. Lima's beautifully warm hat, it might not be so bad. I took the hat down from the hook, admiring the thick, expensive fur. I put it on. It hung down past my eyes and ears, and I could immediately feel it's warmth. I quietly opened the door, turned on my flashlight, and headed through the wind to the outhouse.

Entering the outhouse, I set my flashlight down beside me and braced myself for the shock of the freezing cold toilet seat. Thank goodness for the extra warmth of Mr. Lima's expensive fur hat. When I was done, I stood up and reached for my flashlight, and then it happened. The oversized hat slipped off my head and fell straight into the toilet, landing with a resounding plop at the bottom of the deep hole.

"Aaaaaagh!" I wailed. I was doomed. With dread, I aimed my flashlight into the hole and spotted the hat lying on a pile of.....well, you know what. The hat was way too far down the hole to reach. I didn't know what to do, so I headed back through the cold and into the cabin. Tiptoing past Mr. Lima's room, I decided to wake Gordon and Paulo to break the news to them. They sat up groggily when I shook them, but after I told them what had happened, they were both suddenly wide awake.

"My dad's hat? His expensive, genuine beaver fur hat? It's at the bottom of the outhouse?" asked Paulo in disbelief.

"I can't believe it's happened again! That hat must be cursed," yawned Gordon.

"The first thing we need to do is get the hat out of the outhouse and see how bad it is," said Paulo.

"But how will we get it out?" I cried. "I can't reach it!"

But Gordon had an idea. He and Paulo quickly

dressed, and the three of us tiptoed back down the hall, past Mr. Lima snoring peacefully (and unsuspectingly) in his bed, and we grabbed our coats and boots. Gordon reached over and picked up a fishing rod on the way out.

We crowded into the outhouse and I shone my flashlight down the hole. Gordon lowered the lure into the hole and snagged the hat on the hook. He slowly and carefully reeled in the hat, and then our worst fears were confirmed; The hat stunk. I grabbed it on its clean side and unhooked the lure. We took the hat outside and rubbed the dirty side in some unmelted snow.

"Did I ever tell you the story of the rabbit and the bear?" asked Gordon.

Paulo shot us a look. "Shut up, Gordon. This is no time for jokes!"

I gave the hat a quick sniff. It stunk. We carried it back into the cabin, where we spent two hours washing and rinsing the hat until it was clean and shiny again. We then carefully dried it out over the wood stove. Just as the sun was starting to come up, we hung the hat back on its hook by the door and tiptoed into bed. A few minutes later, the alarm clock went off in Mr. Lima's room. We listened with impending dread as Paulo's dad got up, dressed, and crossed the cabin to the back door, where he put on his coat, boots and his expensive, genuine beaver fur hat. We heard the door open and shut as Mr. Lima headed off to the outhouse.

So far, so good.

Two minutes later, the cabin door swung open and Mr. Lima stormed in, slamming the door behind him.

"Get up, you guys. Right now. Alright, which one of you did it?" yelled Mr. Lima.

Oh-oh, I thought. *We've been caught!* We filed out into the kitchen, where Mr. Lima stood fuming, still wearing his hat.

Holding his fishing rod in his hand, he bellowed, "Which one of you clowns put my good graphite fishing rod in the outhouse?!"

Chapter 5

The Happy Face Affair

It was the first week of May. Birds were nesting, flowers were blooming and our music teacher, Miss Drone, had lost her mind. For weeks, she had been trying to teach our class a new song called "Put On A Happy Face". It was the perfect song for spring, she said, oblivious to the fact that the whole class, and probably the whole school, hated it. We mixed up the words, sang off-key on purpose, and frowned through the whole song, but Miss Drone failed to notice.

"What a stupid song," complained Gordon at recess.

"It's for babies!"

"Yeah," said Paulo. "Who does she think we are, kindergarten kids?"

"Whoever heard of such dumb words?" scowled Gordon.

"'*Spread sunshine all over the place; Just put on a happy face!*'" I sang at the top of my lungs and very off-key. My voice is bad enough at the best of times, and Gordon and Paulo fell down laughing.

"Hey," said Gordon, sitting up. "I've got an idea. If Miss Drone wants happy faces, then it's happy faces she'll get!"

Gordon pulled a black marker from his pocket and marched over to one of the school doors. Near the handle, he drew a small happy face. Paulo and I snickered. What a great idea!

We spent the rest of the day drawing happy faces all over the school when no one was looking. We drew them on garbage cans and desks, on the blackboard, and even a small one on the side of the school bus.

Before school the next day, Gordon slipped into the

gym with his marker. When the class filed in for phys ed, there was shouting and laughter as kids discovered a large smiling face on every single basketball.

Later that day, the principal interrupted classes with a special announcement. He said that happy faces had been discovered all over the school, and that the person or persons responsible must stop immediately or face severe punishment. Finally, anyone who knew anything about these happy faces was asked to report to the office.

By this time, I was getting a little nervous, but Gordon didn't bat an eye during the entire announcement. That's Gordon - cool as a cucumber.

When our bus pulled in to the school yard the next day, there were even more happy faces everywhere - on the swings, on the monkey bars, and even on the windows. Apparently, the principal's announcement had given every kid in the school the same idea.

Another special announcement was made immediately after the morning bell. Anyone caught defacing school property with happy faces would be expelled!

Extra custodians had to be hired to help wash the

hundreds of happy faces off of walls and doors, but a couple of custodians working overtime were no match for hundreds of kids.

Miss Drone must have seen the connection between her song and our happy faces, because we no longer had to sing "Put On A Happy Face" in music class.

"Well, boys. My work here is done," said Gordon with satisfaction. "We can stop drawing happy faces."

"Sure," said Paulo. "But how are you gonna get everyone else to stop?"

"That's easy," replied Gordon. "Sooner or later, someone will get caught, and that will be the end of it."

The end came sooner than we expected. At recess that afternoon, the principal himself came out for yard duty. His eyes darted furiously around the school yard as he tried to catch the guilty party in the act of drawing a happy face.

The hundreds of happy faces drawn all over the school had not gone unnoticed by anyone, even the littlest kindergarten students, who loved the happy faces. They even loved the happy face song. As the principal roamed the yard searching for the culprit, he spied a little girl with a purple crayon clutched in her fist. The little girl raised her crayon to the wall of the school and innocently drew a tiny purple happy face.

"A-ha!" cried the principal triumphantly. He flew across the yard. "Now I've got you!!" Every kid in the school yard froze and stared at the principal.

"NO-O-O-O!" came a loud shout from one of the on-lookers. *It was Gordon!* "I drew all those happy faces! It wasn't her. It was me!" Gordon raced across the yard to cut off the principal before he reached the girl, who was none other than Gordon's little sister.

The principal stopped and looked at Gordon, and then at his little sister, and then back at Gordon.

Shaking his head, he said, "I should've known that a kindergarten student couldn't possibly be guilty of such a thing. *You*, on the other hand," he said turning to Gordon, "could be guilty of *anything!*"

Gordon was promptly marched to the principal's office, where he was given a pail, a sponge and a bottle of detergent. He was forced to spend the next two days scrubbing off every happy face in the entire school. As if that weren't bad enough, he also had to apologize to Miss Drone, who made Gordon stand in front of the whole class and sing "Put On A Happy Face".

Chapter 6

The Bear

It was the long weekend and Gordon's Uncle Ivan was taking the three of us to his cabin in the woods. Uncle Ivan's new wife Jennifer had decided that Uncle Ivan should see for himself what fun having kids would be before they started a family of their own. Aunt Jennifer had pleaded with us, begged us and bribed us to be on our best behaviour that weekend to help convince Uncle Ivan that he really wanted kids.

"Whatever you do," she warned us, "be careful in that cabin. It's your uncle's favourite place in the whole world. He even wanted to spend our honeymoon there!"

With promises not to destroy the cabin and to be on our best behaviour, we climbed into Uncle Ivan's four-by-four truck and headed off for three days of fishing, hunting and adventure in the woods.

Although it was a four hour drive to the cabin, not once did we ask that famous bored-kid-in-the-backseat question, "Are we there yet?" Not once did Gordon, Paulo or I clutch our stomachs and say in a weak voice "I'm sta-a-a-rving. When are we going to eat?" Not once did we fight over who got to sit in the front seat. It was the longest four hours three kids ever spent in a vehicle, but we were determined to show Uncle Ivan how quiet and peaceful driving with three boys could be. Aunt Jennifer would have been impressed.

Finally we pulled up in front of a small cabin at the end of a long, rutted dirt road. "Well, here we are at last," announced Uncle Ivan. "No neighbours for miles. Just you and me and the mosquitoes." We scrambled out of the truck and ran toward the front door. The cabin had one main room that served as a kitchen and living room, two small bedrooms and a back door leading to the outhouse. Uncle Ivan went around opening windows to air out the cabin while Gordon, Paulo and I unpacked. We would share one of the bedrooms. We didn't fight over who got to sleep beside the window, or who would get the top bunk.

Several times during the day, Uncle Ivan asked if we were feeling alright. We smiled and said "Yes, sir. We're just fine."

Later that afternoon as we quietly assembled our fishing rods in the living room, Uncle Ivan informed us that he had forgotten to bring coffee. "And I'm a bear without my morning coffee. I'm just going to run into town and get some, boys. Will you be OK without me for a while?"

"Of course," we chorused.

"Maybe we'll take a nature hike while you're gone," said Paulo.

"Drive carefully, Uncle Ivan," Gordon added

thoughtfully. The minute the truck was out of sight, we let out a long sigh of relief.

"Man," said Gordon. "All this politeness is killing me!"

"Yeah," I agreed. Let's have some real fun before he gets back."

We grabbed our fishing gear and raced down to the dock. Peering over the side into the water, Gordon shouted,

"Hey, guys! Look at the size of that bass!" Paulo and I leaned over the water, peering into the depths. Suddenly from behind, I felt a hand pushing me, and Paulo and I both went over the side of the dock and into the chilly water. We came up sputtering and furious, while Gordon laughed hysterically on the dock. Paulo and I raced up the ladder, but Gordon was already off and running toward the forest at top speed, knowing full well what would happen to him when we caught him. Paulo and I sloshed after him, dripping water and shouting. Gordon was laughing so hard he could hardly run, and soon we had almost caught up to him. Frantically he looked over his shoulder to see us gaining on him, and then it happened. Gordon tripped over a large mound of dirt on the forest floor. As he lay there, stunned, the mound of dirt rose up and growled! Paulo and I slammed on the brakes! We stood with our mouths hanging open, eyes wide with fear. The mound of dirt was actually *a sleeping bear!* Pandemonium broke out. There was shouting and screaming. Gordon sprang to his feet and began running toward Paulo and me, ready to take his chances with us rather than the bear. All three of us turned tail and sprinted toward the cabin with the bear in hot pursuit. Paulo reached the cabin first and flung open the door. The four of us dashed inside and fell to the ground, gasping and exhausted. *The four of us?!* The bear had followed us into the cabin! In one fluid motion, Gordon, Paulo and I jumped up and flew out of the cabin, slamming the door behind us and trapping the bear inside. We fell to the ground, hearts racing, but safe at last.

For a moment, all was silent inside the cabin, and then we heard it - a loud crash, followed by a deep, angry growl and the sound of splintering wood. The bear was destroying Uncle Ivan's prized cabin! With growing alarm, we realized that we would be blamed for letting the bear inside.

"Aunt Jennifer's gonna kill us!" moaned Gordon.

"Kill *us*?" I shrieked. "*You're* the one who tripped over the bear. And *you're* the one who forgot to close the door. *You* let the bear into the cabin, not us!"

Dejectedly, we looked at one another. We were supposed to be on our best behaviour, and in less than one hour we had destroyed Uncle Ivan's cabin.

"Well, we can't let the bear out. He'll only come after us again," said Paulo matter-of-factly.

"Yeah," I agreed. "Let's go pick up our rods and decide what to do." Silently, we headed toward the dock. Just when we thought things couldn't get any worse, we heard Uncle Ivan's truck coming up the rutted road. We froze, not knowing what to do. The truck door slammed.

"We can't let him go into the cabin with the bear," cried Paulo. "Come on!" We grabbed our fishing gear and ran back to the cabin just as Uncle Ivan swung open the front door. We were too late.

In a flash, the bear was on Uncle Ivan, and the two of them fell to the ground. There was growling and roaring and cursing. The two fighters tumbled and swung at each other. The dust was flying, and when it cleared, we saw Uncle Ivan holding the bear in a headlock.

"Run, boys!" he shouted, but we were rooted to the spot. Suddenly, the bear gave a great shake and broke free. For one long terrible moment, the bear and Uncle Ivan stood eyeing each other warily, and then without warning, the bear turned around and ambled back into the forest behind the cabin. Gordon, Paulo and I ran up to Uncle Ivan.

"Are you OK?" shouted Paulo.

"Are you bleeding?" I demanded.

"Wow! That was awesome!" exclaimed Gordon.

Uncle Ivan did not appear hurt, but he was shaken up by the ordeal. "Thank heavens you boys weren't in the cabin when that *%sh#@* bear got in! He must have come in through my bedroom window!"

Gordon, Paulo and I exchanged glances, silently agreeing that there was no point in telling Uncle Ivan the truth about how the bear really got into the cabin. After all, Aunt Jennifer would have wanted it that way.

Chapter 7

The Mayor's Garden

The mayor of our town lives in a big mansion on a hill and is one of the richest men in town. The driveway is over half a kilometer long. The front lawn is perfectly manicured and filled with fancy flower gardens and water fountains. There are goldfish ponds, tall stately maple trees, and sculptured bushes. Gordon, Paulo and I have ridden by the mayor's house dozens of times. The property is surrounded by a high fence with NO TRESPASSING signs, and rumour had it that the mayor kept vicious guard dogs. It was also believed that the mayor did not like children. This, we found out, was true.

It was Tuesday morning and Gordon, Paulo and I were on our bikes, heading for the river to see if last night's heavy rain had improved the fishing. We were huffing and puffing our way up the long, steep hill near the mayor's house, when we spotted his large black car turning out of the driveway. The car headed towards us as we made our way up the incline, and just as it passed us, the car hit a puddle, spewing a tidal wave of cold, muddy water onto Gordon, Paulo and me. We were soaked from head to foot! We stopped our bikes and stared at each other in disbelief. It was Paulo who finally spoke first.

"I can't believe it!" he shouted, a fat worm falling from his hair. "That guy splashed us on purpose! He's probably laughing his head off right now."

"No. He couldn't be that mean," I said in disbelief. "It must have been an accident."

As if on cue, the large car stopped and began backing up.

"See," I whispered. "Here he comes now to apologize." When the big car reached us, one dark tinted window slid down. The three of us leaned forward in anticipation of an apology. Instead, we were hit with a huge puff of cigar smoke, and then the mayor's grinning face as he said,

"Enjoy your shower, boys? Ha! Ha! Ha!" With that, the mayor stepped on the accelerator, sending more muddy water our way as he roared out of sight. We stood there, not knowing what to do. The mayor had soaked us on purpose! It was unbelievable.

We cancelled our fishing plans and pedalled to our clubhouse in my backyard to decide what to do. After talking about it and arguing for half an hour, we realized that there wasn't anything we *could* do. After all, he was the mayor, and we were just kids.

"Who's gonna believe *us*?" I said. That guy's gonna get away with splashing us and there is not a thing we can do about it."

"Maybe there is, and maybe there isn't," mused Gordon. "The police won't believe us, and our parents sure as heck won't believe us." Then a gleam came into Gordon's eyes. "Boys," he said with a cunning smile, "it looks like it's up to us to get even."

"Stop right there, Gordon!" Paulo said. "I'm not going to do anything to get in trouble. I'm tired of being grounded because of your stupid ideas!"

"That's the beauty of my plan, boys," said Gordon smoothly. "We don't have to do anything to the mayor. The mayor will pay himself back. Let me explain."

Gordon told us his scheme to teach the mayor a lesson he would never forget, and we had to agree that it was a good plan. It was better than good. It was beautiful. It was brilliant. Best of all, it was foolproof.

First, we rode our bikes to the dump where we spent the rest of the morning sifting through garbage looking for an old bottle. Not just any bottle would do.

"Hey, here's one!" Paulo finally cried out, holding up a dirty bottle with a rusty metal screw cap still in place.

Back at our clubhouse, equipped with paper and pencil, we set to work on Phase Two of our plan. While Gordon dictated, I wrote:

To the Finder of this Note -
I have buried all of my life savings ten feet behind the big maple tree in this yard.
Signed: Alfred Thomas, 1931

I carefully rolled the note up, slid it in the dirty bottle and replaced the rusty cap.

"Okay," said Paulo. "But how do we get the mayor to find the bottle?"

"That's easy," said Gordon. "All we need is a shovel." We found a small shovel in my garage, strapped it to Gordon's bike and pedaled off in the direction of the mayor's house.

Stashing our bikes in the ditch across the road from his yard, we ran across the road and climbed under the fence, ignoring the NO TRESPASSING signs. We kept a sharp eye out for any sign of the mayor's guard dogs. At the first garden we came to, Gordon made a small hole with the shovel and I dropped the bottle into it. We replaced the dirt, being careful to leave the top of the bottle visible above the earth a little bit. The trap had been set. Now all we had to do was wait for the mayor to spring it.

Every day for the next week and a half we rode our bikes past the mayor's house, looking for signs that he had found the bottle. We were just about to give up hope, and then it happened. We saw what we had been waiting for.

"Look!" yelled Paulo, pointing to a large maple tree near the edge of the mayor's property. Sure enough, ten feet behind the tree was a deep hole and a mound of dirt beside it. We stopped and stared.

"There!" cried Gordon, pointing to another tree where a mound of dirt rose up behind it. There could be no doubt about it. The mayor had found our note!

In the weeks that followed, the number of holes in the mayor's picture-perfect yard increased until one day we counted 23 holes! The fish ponds were full of dirt. The beautiful gardens were ruined, and the lawn looked like a battle ground.

"There he is!" I whispered, pointing to the mayor as he frantically dug another hole.

"Look at him sweat," said Gordon.

The mayor was knee-deep in a hole and he wore the crazed expression of a hungry gold-digger. Our plan had worked! The mayor had paid *himself* back for splashing us, and for once, we didn't even get caught.

Chapter 8

The Class Trip

The school year was winding down and our teacher, Mrs. Hoagsbrith, had placed a large box with a slot in the top on her desk. Across the front was written "Class Trip Suggestions" and students had been dropping in folded up pieces of paper all week. Now Mrs. Hoagsbrith had them spread out all around her and she was reading them aloud to the class and tallying them on a piece of paper. Students were only supposed to make one suggestion each, but oddly enough, there were 45 slips of paper on the teacher's desk and only 24 kids in the class. Mrs.

Hoagsbrith demanded to know who had filled out all the extra suggestions, but we just tried to look innocent and shrugged our shoulders. The teacher sighed and resumed counting.

"Another vote for the zoo, and here's one to go to the water park," she said as she marked our suggestions down. Suddenly she frowned and said, "Very funny. We are NOT going on a tour of the jail." Then she mumbled, "Although some of you may end up there on your own one day!"

There were suggestions to go bowling and to see a play, and four more to go to the jail. Mrs. Hoagsbrith shot Gordon a suspicious glance.

Unfolding another piece of paper, she asked, "Which one of you suggested going to see an autopsy?" We all glanced around, but no hands were raised.

Finally Mrs. Hoagsbrith announced that she thought the zoo would make a lovely end-of-the-year trip. This brought cheers and moaning, and a few kids banged on their desks. The date was set for two weeks from Tuesday.

On the walk home from school, Gordon was particularly glum.

"What I don't get is why we have to drive for three hours on a bus just to look at some dumb animals behind bars when the jail is full of people behind bars. And why do we have to study animals brought in from all over the world while we ignore our own native animals?

"What do you mean?" I asked. Personally, I was looking forward to the zoo.

"Well, right here in Canada is the world's largest meat-eater, the polar bear, but we aren't taught a thing about it. We have to go to the zoo to see Australia's Koala bear, and it isn't even a real bear! It just doesn't make any sense at all!" Gordon was really wound up now.

As the days went on, Gordon continued to complain about our upcoming trip, but two days before we were to go, he announced to Paulo and me,

"I've decided that I'm not going to study and learn about any of those zoo animals. Instead, I'm going to let the zoo animals study and learn about me!" He wouldn't say exactly what he was planning, but Paulo and I promised to help. It was a promise we would soon regret.

On Tuesday we arrived at school two hours early to begin the long drive to the zoo. Even though Paulo and I begged and pleaded, Gordon wouldn't tell us what he planned to teach the animals.

"You guys would chicken out if I told you and you promised to help," he said. Frankly, I was starting to get a little nervous.

At last the bus pulled up at the zoo entrance and we scrambled off to get in line at the ticket booth. The zoo was going to be packed with all kinds of kids and parents on class trips that day, but we were the first to arrive. As soon as we had been put into a group with a parent, Gordon whispered to Paulo and me,

"Come on! Follow me." We ducked out of the group and raced up a path with a sign pointing toward the Monkey House.

Once inside the Monkey House, we stopped to catch our breath, and Paulo said,

"O.K. What's the big plan, Gordon? Spill it!"

Smiling mischievously, Gordon said, "You guys know

how monkeys are supposed to be so smart, right?" We nodded. "Well," continued Gordon. "We're going to teach them a little trick!" And with that, Gordon unzipped his jeans, dropped his pants and mooned all the monkeys in the Monkey House! Paulo and I stared, not knowing quite what to do.

"Come on, guys. You promised!" cried Gordon. So Paulo and I reluctantly dropped our shorts and began mooning the monkeys, too.

"Look, monkeys!" shouted Gordon, making monkey sounds and wagging his bare butt at the cages. We quickly had the attention of every monkey, and soon a few of them began bending over and screeching and dancing around their cages. As more and more monkeys joined in, Gordon cried,

"It's working! The monkeys are mooning us!!"

"Let's get out of here before somebody catches us," said Paulo. We zipped up and ran out of the Monkey House, laughing hysterically. Halfway down the path we ran into our group.

"There you are!" said a very relieved-looking parent.

"We've been searching everywhere. We're supposed to be over at the elephant area."

Still chuckling, we joined the group and marched off to see the elephants. When we arrived, Mrs. Hoagsbrith was reading all about elephants from a brochure.

"Who can tell me the difference between an African elephant and an Asian elephant?" she asked. Several hands shot in the air. Gees, this was as bad as being at school.

On and on we continued through the zoo, moving slowly from one exhibit to the next. Gordon, Paulo and I were too excited with anticipation to pay much attention to anything, but when we finally headed down the path to the Monkey House, we were suddenly very interested. Reading from her brochure, Mrs. Hoagsbrith informed us about the various types of monkeys we would see and that they were highly intelligent creatures who learned very quickly.

No kidding, I thought. Gordon elbowed me in the ribs, laughing.

As we approached the Monkey House, another group

of students was just leaving. They were laughing and carrying on about the monkeys.

"They must have been doing some cute tricks for those students," said one parent innocently. "This should be fun!"

You can say that again, I thought. And then it happened.

We filed into the Monkey House and to our complete delight, the monkeys were all showing off their latest trick. The whole class stared in disbelief as hundreds of monkeys bent over and wiggled their rear ends at us. Everywhere you looked, there were mooning monkeys! The class roared with laughter. Even the parents couldn't help laughing.

"Look at the monkeys!" everyone shouted. The louder we got, the more excited the monkeys became, too, until they were shrieking so loudly we had to cover our ears and run out of the Monkey House.

Kids collapsed on the ground, clutching their stomachs and laughing, but none as hard as Gordon, Paulo and me.

Several zoo keepers came running over to investigate

the big commotion. When they saw the mooning monkeys, they immediately closed the Monkey House until the poor monkeys could be calmed down and taught to behave themselves again.

That was one class trip we would never forget.

Chapter 9

Night Visitor

June ended and school was finally out. Gordon, Paulo and I were looking forward to two glorious months of hanging out and doing nothing. On the last day of school, Gordon managed to talk his parents into letting Paulo and me sleep over at his house. His mother actually seemed pleased when we asked if we could sleep in the backyard in Gordon's pup tent.

"Of course you can, boys. I'm sure you'll have much more fun outside than cooped up in the house with us girls." Gordon had four sisters. What Mrs. Smith really meant was; "Thank goodness I won't have three rowdy boys keeping us awake half the night and messing up the house." Whatever her reasons, we were thrilled.

"Maybe you'd like to have the dog keep you company, too," she added hopefully. Gordon had his very own pup tent, given to him by his Uncle Ivan when he had bought a new one. It was one of Gordon's most prized possessions.

Right after supper, Paulo and I biked over to Gordon's house, loaded down with everything necessary for a great camp-out: sleeping bags, pillows, flashlights, fishing magazines, comic books and a week's allowance worth of candy and pop.

Eager to get the camp-out started, we decided to set up our gear in the tent right away. Rolling out our sleeping bags in the tiny pup tent, we realized it was somewhat smaller than we remembered. But after half an hour of jostling and elbowing each other, we were finally set up. Gordon and I would be sleeping side by side facing the door, and Paulo, who was the shortest, would be sleeping crosswise at our feet. Where Chopper would sleep was left undecided.

We sat on our sleeping bags and leafed through our fishing magazines, recalling recent fishing trips and planning future ones. We talked about the ones that got away, the ones we would surely catch next time, and the new lures we were going to put on our Christmas lists. After a short time, Paulo announced he was hungry, and we opened up the candy we had brought.

"This is better than Halloween," I said, tossing a chocolate bar wrapper over my shoulder and reaching for a bag of chips.

With his mouth full of gummy candies, Gordon said, "Hey, guys, it's getting dark. Let's tell ghost stories!"

"Yeah!" we replied eagerly, and for the next hour we attempted to scare each other with stories of severed heads, one-eyed ghosts, and the famous hook-instead-of-a-hand story. Chills were running up my spine when all of a sudden, from outside the tent, I thought I heard footsteps.

It's just my imagination, I told myself. *No one else*

heard it...NO, THERE IT IS AGAIN! This time Gordon and Paulo heard it, too, for they both froze and we stared at each other. Chopper let out a low growl. We all held our breath, waiting, and then we heard it.

"Boys, the girls and I ordered pizza. I hope you're still hungry!" *It was only Mrs. Smith.* Our snacks had run out half an hour ago and all those ghost stories had stirred up quite an appetite. With Chopper's help, the four of us devoured the pizza, and Chopper even downed half a glass of pop before anybody noticed and stopped him.

When most of the food was gone, we pushed the empty plate, cups and wrappers out of the cramped tent, and settled into our sleeping bags. Almost immediately, I fell asleep with Chopper on my legs.

Sometime during the night, half groggy with sleep, I heard Gordon unzipping the tent to let Chopper out to relieve himself. Too much pop, I guess. A few minutes later he was back, sniffing and pawing through the candy wrappers on the other side of the tent. Lazily, I reached for the zipper and let Chopper back in. That's when I first noticed the stripe of white fur down Chopper's back.

"Hey, Gordon," I mumbled. "What happened to – OH,
MY GOSH! SKUNK!"

Instantly we were fully awake. The tiny pup tent
came to life as the three of us rolled over each other in a
frantic attempt to get untangled from our sleeping bags
and out the rear door. The tent shook violently and the
tent pegs were uprooted. And then it happened. In our
mad scramble to get out someone stepped on the skunk!
A stench like burning rubber suddenly hit my nostrils,
causing me to gag and my eyes to water.

"I'm gonna puke!" croaked Paulo, clutching his throat.

"Not in my tent!" shouted Gordon.

"The zipper's stuck!" I cried.

Hearing the commotion, Gordon's dad raced out of the
house still in his boxer shorts and undershirt to break up
what he figured was a major fight among us boys. His
sisters, also awakened by the racket, lined up at the
kitchen window to watch the spectacle, mouths and eyes
wide open. As the tent bobbed and sprang all over the
back yard like a Whack-A-Mole game at a carnival,
Gordon's dad tackled it, while inside the tent, we

61

continued to claw, scream and fight to get out. Chopper, thinking this was all a game, barked and leapt around Gordon's dad's feet, adding to the commotion.

"BREAK IT UP, YOU GUYS!" ordered Mr. Smith.

With one hand he held the tiny tent down, while the other hand reached inside, clutching wildly. He grabbed hold of what he must have assumed was the hair on one of our heads, and hauled it out of the tent. To his astonishment, he found himself staring into the frightened eyes of the poor skunk. With lightning speed, Mr. Smith dropped the skunk, but not soon enough to avoid being drenched in skunk spray. His face turned the colour of tomato soup, and he began shouting at the top of his lungs.

Holding their noses, Gordon's sisters were quickly ushered back to bed by Mrs. Smith, who returned moments later armed with a pail, several sponges and a bottle of dishwashing soap. The four of us were ordered to strip to our underwear, except for Mr. Smith, who was already in his boxers, and Mrs. Smith hosed us down with icy water in the back yard. Mr. Smith was forced to spend the rest of the night camping out with us in the garage.

As for Gordon's prized pup tent, it had to be burned.

Chapter 10

The Rabbit

It was a beautiful summer day. My best friends, Gordon and Paulo, were at my house helping me get my fishing tackle ready so we could go fishing in the river.

"Come on," I said when we were finally ready. "We don't want to waste any more time."

We headed outside to get our bikes, and Gordon whistled for his dog, Chopper, who had been waiting in the yard for us.

"Here, boy!" he yelled. The dog didn't respond.

"Now where could he have gotten to?" demanded Paulo. "We left him right here by our bikes."

As if on cue, Chopper came bounding across the neighbour's lawn with something furry in his mouth.

"Oh, no! I'll bet he's been in Mr. Butterworth's garbage," I said.

The dog trotted up to Gordon and sat down in front of him.

"Hey, that looks like...OH NO!" I yelled. "DROP IT, CHOPPER!" Clenched between the dog's teeth was a rabbit. Chopper dropped the animal at his owner's feet and looked up proudly as if to say, *"Hey, guys. Look what I caught!"*

The rabbit was dead.

"That's Mr. Butterworth's rabbit!" I said in shock. "He loved that rabbit! Now we're really in trouble!" It was a regular sight on our street to see Mr. Butterworth filling his birdfeeders or weeding his gardens with the bunny hopping along after him.

We all scowled at Chopper. Sensing our anger, the dog slunk off and sat beside our tree fort by himself.

"That rabbit sure is muddy," commented Gordon, peering at the dead animal.

"Chopper must have chased him through the garden. Man, are you in trouble. I'll bet your parents won't let you go camping with us next weekend," said Paulo, looking at me.

"*Me?*" I asked in surprise. "It wasn't *my* fault that Gordon's dog killed a rabbit. That's what dogs do. Besides, I'm not the one who left him out here!" I glared at Gordon.

"Don't blame me," said Gordon. "Anyway, I have a plan." Paulo and I groaned, but Gordon insisted that we at least give it a try. "Unless you *want* to get in major trouble and have our trip canceled!" he said.

Paulo and I sighed and listened to Gordon's plan.

First, we took the dead rabbit into the house and gave him a bath in the tub. We used lots of shampoo to get all the dirt out of his fur, and then we rinsed him until all the mud and shampoo were gone. Gordon wiped the rabbit with a big towel. Next, we took my mother's blow-dryer and dried his fur. In a couple of minutes, the rabbit was dry and clean.

"Hey, he looks as good as new!" exclaimed Paulo.

The rabbit did look good with his fur fluffy and gleaming.

Next, we carried the rabbit outside and I snuck around to Mr. Butterworth's garage and peered in through the window. There was no car; The coast was clear.

"Okay. Now all we have to do is put the rabbit on the old man's porch, and Mr. Butterworth will never know that Chopper killed him. He'll think he died of a heart attack or something," said Gordon.

I had to admit it was a good plan. We gently place the dead rabbit by the front door and raced back across the lawn to our bikes. We grabbed our fishing gear and pedaled off down the road toward the river with Chopper running along after us.

"Whew!" said Paulo when we were well away from the house. "I'm glad that's over with. There's *no way* we can get caught!"

"And we can still go camping," I said with a sigh of relief.

We fished unsuccessfully for several hours and at

dinnertime, we each pedaled home to our own houses.

Entering the kitchen, I saw mom making dinner. When she saw me, she exclaimed,

"Have you heard the news?"

"What news?" I asked.

"Mr. Butterworth was just over. He told me that his rabbit died two days ago and he buried it in his back yard. And today, some sicko dug up the rabbit, cleaned it off and put it on his front porch!"

I gulped loudly. *Chopper must have dug up an already-dead rabbit!* Did mom suspect the sicko was really Gordon, Paulo and me?

"With some weirdo running around digging up dead animals, I'm going to make sure the windows and doors are all locked tonight," she continued. "And, oh, by the way. I talked to Gordon and Paulo's parents, and they feel that it wouldn't be safe for you boys to go camping by yourselves next weekend with this weirdo on the loose. I'm afraid you'll have to cancel your trip."

I opened my mouth to protest, but realized that she might not know that it was Gordon, Paulo and me, and every kid knows that you never admit anything you don't have to.

Chapter 11

The Camera

It was summer, and our parents had once again sent Gordon, Paulo and me off to camp. Summer camp is supposed to be a vacation for kids, but we knew better. Our parents felt that two weeks with the three of us gone was a vacation for *them*.

Camp Outback hadn't changed much from last year, and we were kept busy with the usual camp things - fishing, swimming, canoeing, baseball and campouts. We were having a very relaxing time.

One day, when the mail arrived, Gordon received a package from his Uncle Ivan.

"Hey, look what I got," he cried happily. "A disposable camera!"

"Cool!" said Paulo. "Let's go fishing and take pictures of our catch!"

"Nah. That's boring," replied Gordon. "I've only got 12 shots on this camera. I want pictures of things you don't see everyday. Something really different..."

I knew that look on Gordon's face only too well. He was concocting a plan, and that usually meant trouble...and a whole lot of fun! All day we waited for Gordon to tell us what he had planned, but when we went to bed that night, he still hadn't taken a single picture.

The next morning, Gordon woke Paulo and me early and said,

"Come with me, and *be quiet*."

We slid silently out of bed and followed Gordon out of the cabin and down the path that led to the outhouse. In his hands, Gordon clutched his disposable camera. When we reached the outhouse, Gordon motioned for us to hide

71

in the bushes, and then he tiptoed quietly up to the door. He waited for a moment, and then he grabbed the handle and yanked the door open. The kid inside opened his mouth in surprise.

"Say '*cheese!*'" shouted Gordon, and before the poor kid had time to react, Gordon snapped his picture. The three of us raced off down the path back to our cabin, laughing hysterically.

"Did you see the look on that kid's face?!" demanded Gordon. "Sitting there like that wearing nothing but a t-shirt and a smile!"

"He's gonna kill you," I said.

"Yeah," Paulo agreed. "You'd better hide that camera before he gets a hold of it and yanks out the film."

"I'm not worried," said Gordon coolly. "No one's gonna get this camera from me. I intend to have some real fun!"

Paulo and I just looked at each other. By now the other campers were awake, demanding to know what the noise was all about.

"Oh, nothing," said Gordon. "We just went on a little

nature walk this morning!" and we burst out laughing again.

All morning, Paulo and I kept waiting for Gordon to take another picture. Even though I felt sorry for the kid in the outhouse, I was secretly dying to know who Gordon would capture next on film. I could hardly concentrate on the baseball game we were playing, and twice I missed the ball when it was hit in my direction. Then, just as we were coming in from the field for our last turn at bat, Gordon motioned to Paulo and me, and we followed him toward the camp pool.

"They're just finishing their swimming lesson," said Gordon, pointing to a group of boys from another cabin. "We'll wait until they're in the change room and then surprise them!"

Paulo laughed, but I was getting a little worried. There were a lot of kids in there, and they might not enjoy getting their pictures taken in the buff.

As soon as the last camper made his way into the change room, Gordon counted to ten and then ran inside and yelled,

"Smile, everyone!"

A second later he was back outside and tearing off down the path into the woods.

When Paulo and I caught up with him, he was doubled over with laughter. Tears streamed down his face.

"You should've seen them. All standing there with nothing on. They were too surprised to cover up. This picture will be even better than the first one."

"They're gonna come after you," I warned.

"No they won't. And besides, I'm gonna hide this camera right here in the woods." And with that, Gordon climbed the nearest tree and tucked the camera into a crook between two branches.

"They'll never find it there," he said, jumping down. The three of us headed back to camp.

That night at dinner, the whole camp was buzzing with news of Gordon's exploits. Because the camera had been in front of Gordon's face, no one knew who the photographer was. One thing was clear, however. Everyone who had had their picture taken wanted revenge - and everyone else thought it was hilarious. I was getting a little nervous.

The next day the whole camp was going on a nature hike in the woods. Gordon got up early and snuck off to get his camera out of the tree, and then hid it in his knapsack. All day I kept waiting for him to strike again, but nothing happened.

"I'm waiting for the perfect moment," he explained to Paulo and me.

"That kid getting stung by the bee in the butt was pretty funny," said Paulo.

"Yeah, but I can do better than that," replied Gordon - and he did.

When we returned to camp, the boy who had been stung hobbled off to the nurse's cabin for a bit of first aid, and Gordon quickly followed him, with Paulo and me right on his heels to catch all the action.

Gordon tiptoed up to the open window of the nurse's cabin, and was delighted to see the boy bent over the examining table, shorts around his ankles, while the nurse pulled out the stinger with a pair of tweezers.

"There," she said when she extracted the stinger.

"Now, just wait here for a minute, and I'll put some ointment on it to take the sting away." The nurse walked over to a cabinet and rummaged through the drawer. Gordon seized the moment.

Click!!

The boy's head jerked around in time to see Gordon's back as he disappeared down the path away from the nurse's cabin.

Even I had to admit that this was beginning to get fun, but I was still nervous. I'm not sure whether I was more afraid of Gordon getting caught and beaten to a pulp by a mob of angry campers, or of getting caught on film in an embarrassing pose myself. Already I was afraid to change into my bathing trunks or use the outhouse. The first problem was easily solved. I wore my bathing suit all the time under my shorts so I couldn't possibly get caught naked. The outhouse problem wasn't so easily solved, and I was starting to get uncomfortable.

As it turned out, I wasn't the only nervous camper. That night at dinner, everyone was talking about ways to avoid using the outhouse.

"Just go in the woods," said one kid. "That way the camera guy can't find you."

That night, I noticed more and more kids heading into the woods clutching rolls of toilet paper in their hands. *Well, why not?* I thought, and I followed them into the woods and chose a nice large shrub. Ahhh, relief. When I got back to our cabin, Gordon laughed and said,

"Don't tell me *you're* scared?"

I didn't reply.

The next day I awoke with the knowledge that I had to use the outhouse *right away.* Something I had eaten for dinner must not have agreed with me; I was cramped up and needed to go *now.* I looked over at Gordon in the next bunk. He was asleep, or at least, he was pretending to be asleep. You couldn't be too careful with Gordon. I silently crept out of my bunk, slid my feet into my running shoes, and tiptoed across the floor. Halfway to the door, the floor creaked loudly and I turned quickly to see if Gordon stirred. He slept on. Once outside the cabin, I raced to the outhouse and grabbed a roll of toilet paper from the hook. I really had to go now.

Just use the outhouse. Don't be such a chicken, I thought. Suddenly, I heard a twig snap behind me, and I turned around, expecting to see Gordon and his camera. I didn't see anyone, but I wasn't going to take any chances. I turned away from the outhouse and ran down the path into the woods. I was ready to explode when I finally reached the far edged of camp near the lake. I looked around frantically for Gordon, but I didn't see him. I peeled off my pyjamas and bathing suit, and squatted to do my business, all the while looking down the path expecting to see Gordon. After several minutes, I stood up, relieved, and pulled on my bathing suit and pyjamas. And then it happened. As I turned around to pick up the roll of toilet paper, I saw a canoe on the lake not 3 metres from me, and in it was a family of four out for some early morning fishing. They stared silently at me, and I stared back, my face turning redder by the second. A mother, a father and two young girls with their mouths open had witnessed the whole thing. I was going to kill Gordon.

I raced back to camp and burst into the cabin.

"Get up, Gordon!" I shouted. He awoke with a start.

"What's wrong?" he mumbled.

"I just went to the bathroom in front of four people, and not just a quick leak either!!" I shouted. "And it's all your fault!"

By now, the whole cabin was awake.

"Why is that my fault?" he asked

"Because, if you hadn't been following people around with that dumb camera waiting to catch them with their pants down, I would've used the outhouse and had some privacy, that's why!"

Gordon began to laugh. "Oh, didn't I tell you? My camera fell out of the tree last night and broke. I threw it in the lake! I won't be taking any more pictures. Sorry, old pal." And he calmly rolled over and went back to sleep.

About the Authors

Michael Wade was born a long time ago, in a place far, far away. He grew up in London, Ontario and currently lives in Strathroy, Ontario. Michael enjoys hunting, wilderness canoeing and working out.

Laura Wade was born not quite so long ago and not as far away as Michael. She, too, was raised in London, Ontario and currently resides in Strathroy, where she works as a Children's Librarian.